This book belongs to

Isabella

Girl on the Go

story by Jennifer Fosberry • pictures by Mike Litwin

sourcebooks jabberwocky

For Valeria and Louise,
who should have gotten to
see more of the world,
and for Bars, who makes
sure that I do.
—JF

For Alora, my
littlest Girl on the Go.
—ML

Published by Sourcebooks Jabberwocky, an imprint of Sourcebooks, Inc.
P.O. Box 4410, Naperville, Illinois 60567-4410
(630) 961-3900
Fax: (630) 961-2168
www.jabberwockykids.com

Library of Congress Cataloging-in-Publication data is on file with the publisher.

Source of Production: Lehigh Phoenix, Rockaway, NJ USA
Date of Production: December 2011
Run Number: 16766

Printed and bound in the United States of America.
PX 10 9 8 7 6 5 4 3 2 1

"Isabella," the father said.
"Where is my favorite little girl?"

"I am NOT a little girl,"
Isabella said.

"Then who is going
to help me today?"
asked the father.

"I am an ARCHEOLOGIST,
searching the hottest, driest desert
for the tomb of a king."

"Well, Isabella, I think you will
DISCOVER that your MUMMY
gave us plenty to do today."

"Okay, Ms. Eagle Eyes,"
the father said.
"Let's go dig some holes."

"I am not an archeologist,"
said the little girl.

"Then who will help
me tend the garden?"
asked the father.

"I am an *artist*, painting the prettiest, glitteriest streets that lead to the tower of lights."

"O la la, Isabella! Now let's head to the Champs de Lettuce."

"Ma petite artiste,"
the father said. "Come and
bring your paintbrush."

"I am not an artist,"
said the little girl.

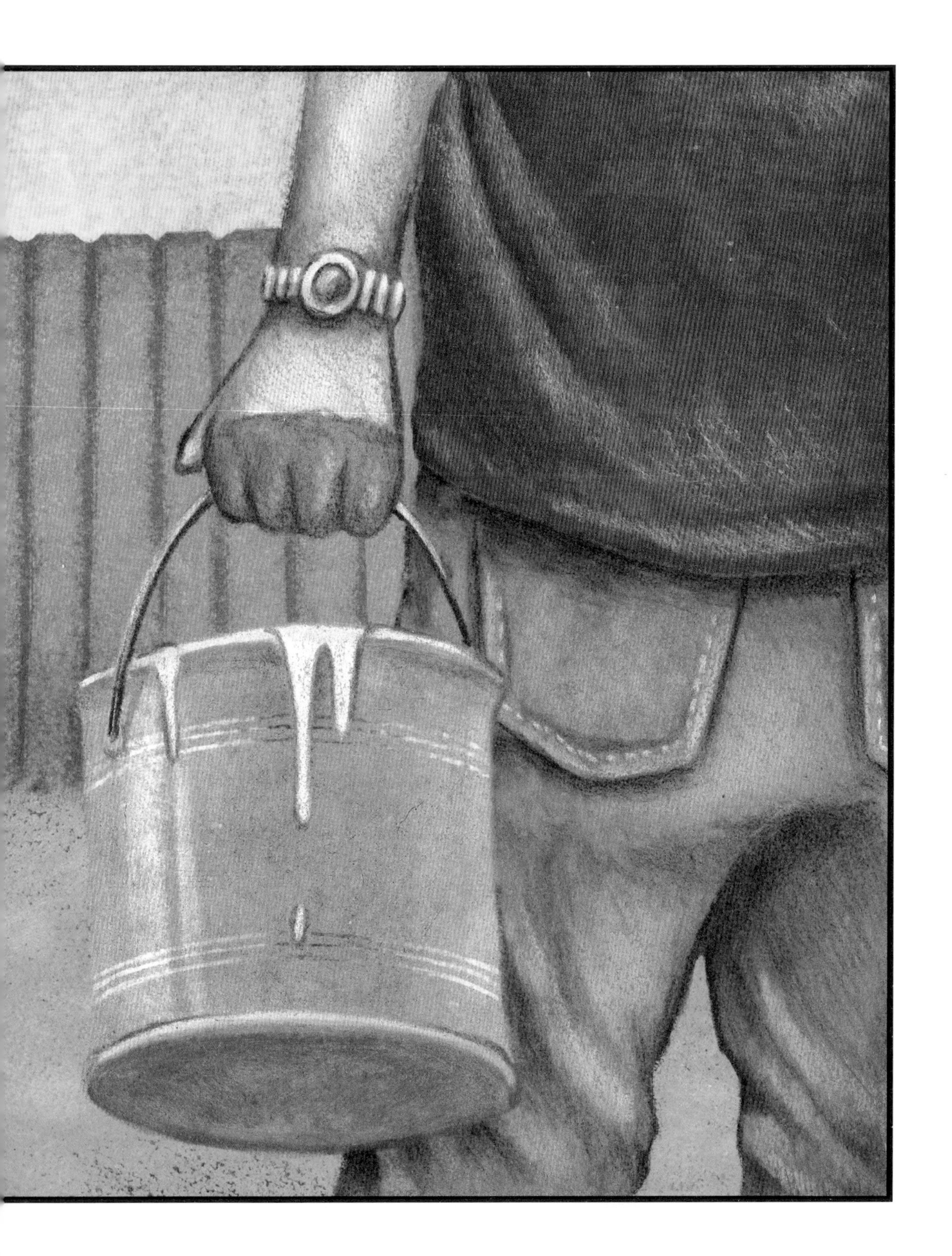

"Then who will help
me paint this fence?"
asked the father.

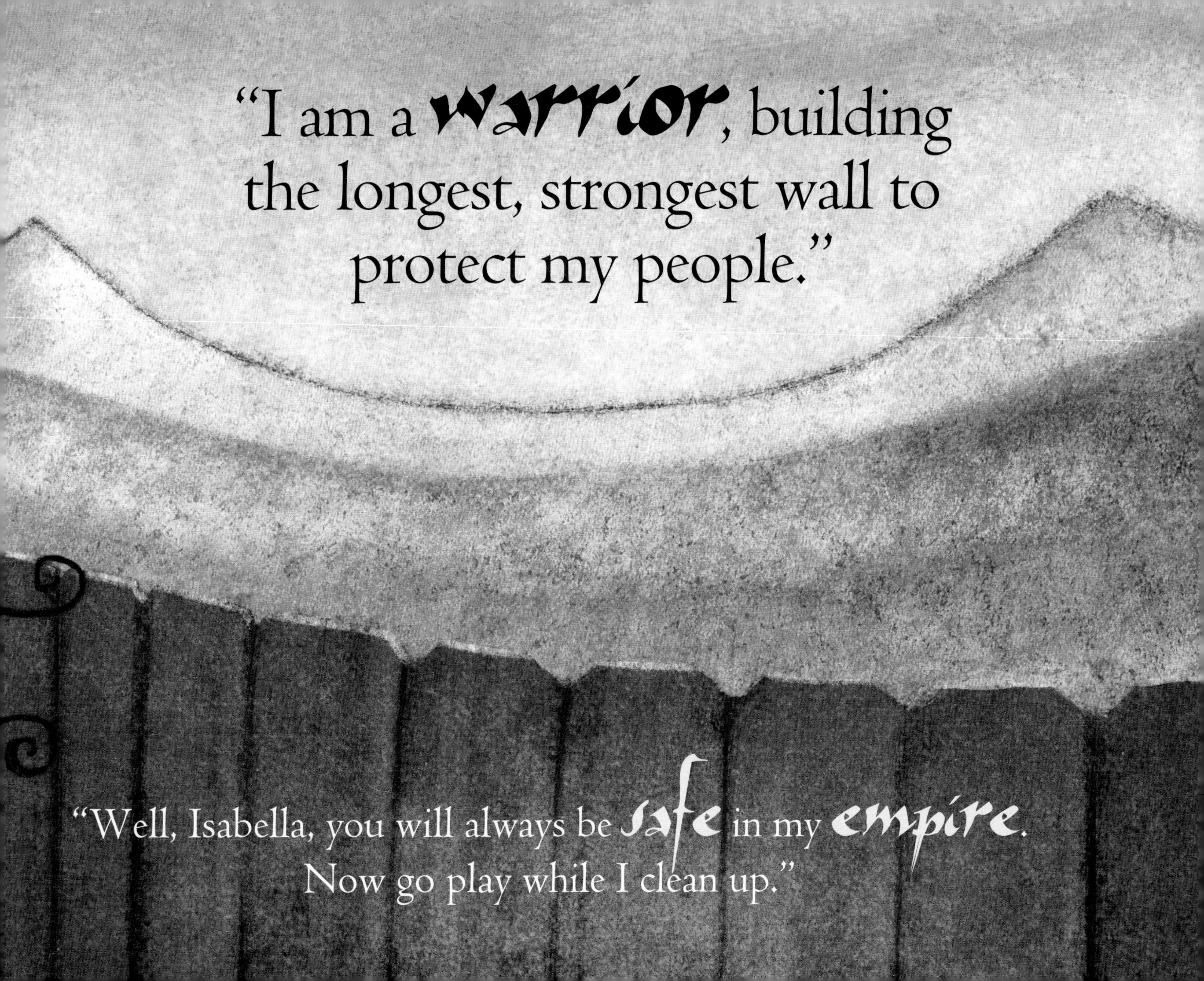

"I am a *warrior*, building the longest, strongest wall to protect my people."

"Well, Isabella, you will always be *safe* in my *empire*. Now go play while I clean up."

"All right, champ," the father said. "Let's get back to work."

"I am not a warrior," said the little girl.

"Then who will help me fix the fort?" asked the father.

"I am an ASTRONOMER,
climbing the oldest, steepest steps
to the top of the Mayan temple."

"Well, Isabella, according to my CALENDAR, we don't have much DAYLIGHT left."

"My little stargazer," the father said. "We have a few minutes left to play."

"I am not an astronomer," said the little girl.

"Then who wants a push on the swing?" asked the father.

"I am **the Queen**,
inspecting the
pendulum on
the greatest,
grandest clock."

"Well, Bells, ticktock.
Five more minutes
and then it's time."

"Your Majesty," the father said. "Grab the flashlight and light the path for us."

"I am not a queen!" said the little girl.

"Then who will lead the way inside?" asked the father.

"I am a defender of **FREEDOM** and I hold the brightest, lightest beacon of **HOPE**."

"Well, **LADY LIBERTY**, let me **ENLIGHTEN** you that it is time for bed."

As they reached the house the father asked, "Isabella, where are we headed now? The Taj Mahal? Maybe the CN Tower?"

"No, Daddy," the little girl said. "I have explored the whole world and I have discovered the most wonderful place."

"And where might
that be, Isabella?"
asked the father.

"Our Home," said the little girl as she took her father's hand and went inside to dream about where she would go...

...tomorrow.

places that changed the world...

PYRAMIDS OF GIZA:

In the hot desert outside Cairo, Egypt, tower three huge pyramids and a giant stone statue that make up the Giza complex. The statue is called the Great Sphinx. It has the body of a lion and the head of a man and it seems to be guarding the pyramids. It is the largest statue ever made from one single stone. The pyramids were built by placing huge stones on top of one another. The stones get smaller as the pyramid gets taller, so the sides look like steps climbing to the point. The largest pyramid was built around 4,500 years ago. It is over 480 feet tall, the size of one and a half football fields! Many of the stones weigh at least three tons, and some of the inner stones weigh as much as eighty tons. (A minivan weighs about two tons.) Scholars still do not know how the ancient Egyptians moved these stones without any machines, but they do know it took a long time to finish—probably twenty years. Pyramids were built for Egypt's leaders, who were called Pharaohs. When they died, the Pharaohs' bodies were made into mummies and placed in the pyramids with things they would need in the afterlife. Of the seven wonders of the ancient world, the largest pyramid at Giza is the only one still standing today.

An **ARCHEOLOGIST** is a person who explores ancient civilizations by studying their buildings and decorations and the items they used every day.

EIFFEL TOWER:

On the Champs de Mars (Field of Mars) in the city of Paris, France, a tall, triangular monument rises high above the pretty, glittery streets. It is the Eiffel Tower and it was built in 1889 as the entrance to the World's Fair. It is eighty-one stories high (or 1,063 feet) and was the tallest structure in the world until the Chrysler Building was built in New York City in 1930. The Eiffel Tower was designed by Gustave Eiffel, whose firm also designed and built the interior iron framework of the Statue of Liberty. It took three hundred workers two years, two months, and five days to assemble the 18,083 pieces of iron that were held together with 2.5 million rivets. It was built out of a special kind of metal called puddled iron. At the time it was built, many Parisians thought the tower was ugly, and they planned to demolish it in 1909. It was saved because it was perfect for sending radio transmissions. Today the Eiffel Tower stands as a beautiful symbol of the city of Paris. It is one of the most visited monuments in the world.

An **ARTIST** is someone who creates things such as paintings and sculptures to portray people, places, objects, emotions, or ideas.

GREAT WALL OF CHINA:

China is one of the world's biggest countries, and in ancient times, many different emperors, or leaders, ruled different parts of it. To protect each territory from invaders, the emperors built huge walls. The first walls were built using a wood form and stamping dirt and gravel inside. In 221 BC, Qin Shi Huang conquered all the different lands of China and brought them together to make one big country. He had these old walls torn down and built a new one to protect China from northern invaders. He used many slaves, and many people died during construction. Very little of that wall remains today, but later Chinese emperors kept rebuilding and adding to the wall to keep China safe. Most of the wall that is left today was built during the Ming Dynasty using bricks. The Great Wall is over 3,700 miles long—that is as long as driving from Los Angeles to New York City and then back to St Louis!

WARRIORS are people who fight or work hard for the honor of their name or their people.

CHICHÉN ITZÁ:

Before Christopher Columbus sailed to the New World, Central America was home to a native people called the Mayans. The Mayans built several great cities including one called Chichén Itzá in what is now Mexico. The name means "at the mouth of the well of the Itzá." The site was chosen for its several cenotes, which are big holes in the ground that hold underground water. The area had no rivers, so the Mayans needed these cenotes for water, and they made many offerings to their gods in thanks. The Chichén Itzá complex has several temples, a palace, a ball court, and an observatory. The Mayans made important contributions in the areas of art, architecture, mathematics, literature, and astronomy. The step pyramid at the center of Chichén shows just how smart the Mayans were. It is called the Temple of Kukulcan, but is often called by its nickname, "El Castillo," the castle. On the spring and fall equinox, the setting sun casts a shadow that lines up perfectly with a statue of a snake head. It looks just like a snake slithering down the staircase of the pyramid! It is believed that this helped the Mayans know it was time to plant crops.

ASTRONOMERS are people that study the stars and outer space.

BIG BEN:

In foggy London, England, a big clock tower stands above the Palace of Westminster. It is the largest four-sided clock tower in the world that chimes the hour. The name Big Ben comes from the huge bell inside the tower. The bell is over seven feet tall and nine feet wide—so big that it did not even fit inside the tower upright! It had to be turned sideways and pulled up to the top, which took more than thirty hours. The clock was designed by Edmund Beckett Denison, who won a competition to prove that he could make a clock that would strike exactly on the hour. He took seven years to finish the clock, and it is still very reliable. To keep it working right, caretakers add or subtract pennies from the clock's pendulum, the part of a clock that swings back and forth. This changes the pendulum's center of mass and makes it swing faster or slower. The clock has been working since 1858 (over 150 years!) and it is recognized around the world as a symbol of London.

A **QUEEN** is the ruler of a country, like the United Kingdom, and she helps run the government.

STATUE OF LIBERTY:

On Liberty Island in New York Harbor stands a green lady as tall as a fifteen-story building. Her formal name is "Liberty Enlightening the World," but most people call her the Statue of Liberty. The statue was a gift to the United States from France to celebrate the 100th anniversary of the signing of the Declaration of Independence. It was designed by Frédéric Auguste Bartholdi in the 1870s and some believe that the statue's face looks like his mother. Gustave Eiffel, the same engineer who designed the Eiffel Tower, built the interior ironwork that supports the sculpture. The statue was built in France, then disassembled into 350 pieces and shipped across the ocean. It was then reassembled on a pedestal built by the United States on the existing star-shaped Fort Wood. The statue's golden torch, which shimmers 300 feet in the air, was often what boat passengers first saw when arriving in New York. For many Americans, Lady Liberty remains a sign of democracy, freedom, and opportunity. Thousands of tourists from all over the world visit the statue every day.

A **DEFENDER** is someone who stands up to protect and guard the ideals that they believe in.

TAJ MAHAL:

One of the most beautiful buildings in the world is located in Agra, India, and it was built for love. In the 1600s, India was ruled by the Islamic Mughals. Their fifteen-year-old prince fell in love with the fourteen-year-old Arjumand Banu Begum, and the couple was engaged and married five years later. Although Arjumand was Shah Jahan's third wife, she was his favorite and constant companion. She became known as Mumtaz Mahal, which means "Jewel of the Palace." In 1631, she died while giving birth to their fourteenth child. Shah Jahan was so sad that he ordered a memorial built for her. A large team of highly skilled architects, 22,000 workers, and 1,000 elephants constructed the Taj Mahal over the next twenty years. They used expensive materials such as white marble and jewels from around the world. Soon after it was completed in 1653, one of Shah Jahan's sons took over as emperor and put his father under house arrest. But Shah Jahan was still able to see the monument from his window. He died in 1666 and is buried next to his wife at the Taj Mahal. Today more than two million people visit the memorial each year.

CN TOWER:

The tallest freestanding tower in the Western Hemisphere is located in Toronto, Canada. Built by the Canadian National Railway in 1976, the CN tower is 1,815 feet tall. More than two million people visit the tower each year. They can stand at the top on a glass floor and look down at the street more than a thousand feet below, eat in the highest revolving restaurant, or walk all the way around the roof of the Sky Pod with nothing to hold on to! The tower is also used for broadcasting TV and radio waves. The LED lights on the outside of the tower are controlled by a computer and change colors for special occasions and events. The CN Tower is one of the seven modern wonders of the world and is a symbol for Canada.

HOME:

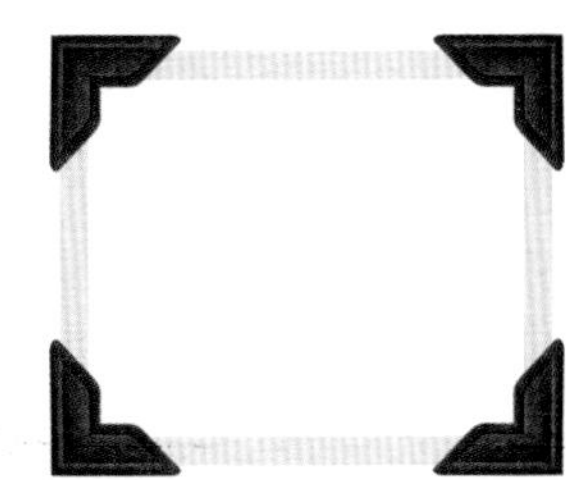

Home is the place where you live with the people that care most about you. It is where you make blanket forts, roller skate in the backyard, play with bubbles in the bathtub, eat homemade chocolate chip pancakes with whipped cream, and read under the covers with a flashlight. It is the place where you feel the most safe and accepted for who you are. It is where you are loved.

acknowledgments

I would like to thank all the people who built amazing, inspiring, and enduring objects of awe. Those who worked with their brains and their backs to create wonderful monuments through feats of engineering and artistry of design. I would also like to thank all the people that helped to put this book into its beautiful, inspiring, and globe-trotting form. For Rebecca Frazer, Kelly Barrales-Saylor, Aubrey Poole, and all the folks at Sourcebooks for inspiration, edits, and direction. For Meredith, Paula, Amy, and Carolyn for listening to a multitude of minute changes, to my family for still believing and supporting, and of course to Mike Litwin for seeing what I saw and making it even better. **–JF**

list of works consulted

On these and other monuments around the world, check out the following:

BOOKS:

Bodden, Valerie. *Pyramids.* Mankato, MN: Creative Education, 2008.

Curlee, Lynn. *Liberty*. New York: Antheneum Books for Young Readers, 2000.

Fisher, Leonard Everett. *The Great Wall of China.* New York: Macmillan, 1986.

Milo, Francesco. *The Story of Architecture.* New York: Peter Bedrick Books, 1999.

Minnis, Ivan. *You Are in Ancient China.* Chicago: Raintree, 2005.

Pezzi, Bryan. *Eiffel Tower.* New York: Weigl, 2008.

Putnam, James and Geoff Brightling and Peter Hayman (photographers). *Pyramid.* London, UK: DK Publishing, 1994.

Singer, Donna. *Structures That Changed the Way the World Looked.* Austin, TX: Raintree Steck-Vaughn, 1995.

Wilkinson, Philip and Paolo Donati and Studio Illibill (illustrators). *Amazing Buildings.* London, UK: Dorling Kindersley, 1993.

WEBSITES:

"Big Ben." New World Encyclopedia. www.newworldencyclopedia.org/entry/Big_Ben.

"Big Ben." UK Parliament. www.parliament.uk/about/living-heritage/building/palace/big-ben.

"Chichén Itzá." Academic Kids. academickids.com/encyclopedia/index.php/Chichen_Itza.

"Chichén Itzá." Chichén Itzá. www.chichenitza.com.

"Chichén Itzá." Mayan Kids. mayankids.com/mmkplaces/mkitza.htm.

"Chichén Itzá." New World Encyclopedia. www.newworldencyclopedia.org/entry/Chichen_Itza.

"CN Tower: 15 Fascinating Facts." About.com Canada Travel. gocanada.about.com/od/canadiancities1/qt/15factscntower.htm.

"Eiffel Tower Facts for Kids." Eiffel Tower Facts. eiffeltowerfacts.org/eiffel-tower-facts-for-kids.

"Eiffel Tower History." Corrosion Doctors. www.corrosion-doctors.org/Landmarks/eiffel-history.htm.

"Eiffel Tower Information." Paris Digest. www.parisdigest.com/monument/toureiffel-stairs.htm.

"Explore the Taj Mahal." Taj Mahal. www.taj-mahal.net/augEng/main_screen.htm.

"Fun Facts about the Statue of Liberty." Statue of Liberty, Ellis Island Foundation, Inc. www.statueofliberty.org/Fun_Facts.html.

"The Giza Archives." Museum of Fine Arts, Boston. www.gizapyramids.org/code/emuseum.asp.

"Giza Pyramids Hold Pharaohs' Ancient Secrets." National Geographic. science.nationalgeographic.com/science/archaeology/giza-pyramids.

"The Great Egyptian Pyramids." Social Studies for Kids. www.socialstudiesforkids.com/articles/worldhistory/pyramids1.htm.

"The Great Pyramid of Giza." Kidsgen. www.kidsgen.com/wonders_of_the_world/pyramid_of_khufu.htm.

"The Great Wall of China." Activity Village. www.activityvillage.co.uk/the_great_wall_of_china.htm.

"The Great Wall of China." Ancient China for Kids. china.mrdonn.org/greatwall.html.

"The Light of Liberty." National Geographic Kids. kids.nationalgeographic.com/kids/stories/history/statue-of-liberty.

"The Pyramids." Kidipede. www.historyforkids.org/learn/egypt/architecture/pyramids.htm.

"Pyramids of Giza." New World Encyclopedia. www.newworldencyclopedia.org/entry/Pyramids_of_Giza.

"Statue of Liberty." Academic Kids. academickids.com/encyclopedia/index.php/Statue_of_Liberty.

"Statue of Liberty Virtual Tour." National Park Service. www.nps.gov/stli/photosmultimedia/virtualtour.htm.

"The Story of Big Ben." Whitechapel Bell Foundry. www.whitechapelbellfoundry.co.uk/bigben.htm.

"Taj Mahal." Academic Kids. academickids.com/encyclopedia/index.php/Taj_Mahal.

"The Taj Mahal." Activity Village. www.activityvillage.co.uk/the_taj_mahal.htm.

"Virtual Chichén." Chichén Itzá. www.mesoweb.com/chichen/virtual/index.html.